KID CARAMEL™

Private Investigator
Book #4

Ghost Ranch
The Legend of Mad Jake

by Dwayne J. Ferguson

Just Us Books, Inc.
East Orange, New Jersey
www.justusbooks.com

Just Us Books, Inc.
356 Glenwood Avenue
East Orange, NJ 07017
www.justusbooks.com

Printed in China
12 11 10 9 8 7 6 5 4
Library of Congress
Cataloging-in-Publication data is available.

ISBN: 0-940975-17-3 (paperback)

He's smart!
He's cool!
He's a detective!
And he's a kid!

The West is indeed wild for kid detective Caramel Parks. Kid Caramel's history teacher has decided to take his students on a class trip to the old western town of Boseville.

Kid is eager to learn more about this historically Black cowboy settlement, especially since Boseville is said to be haunted by a ghost named, "Mad Jake." When the school bus pulls up to a strange sign that says "Hayes's Ranch," Caramel knows the mystery's just begun.

Who is this Mad Jake, and why is he so mad? It doesn't take Kid and his partners too long to find out, but can they give Mad Jake what he wants before it's too late?

Chapter One:
Books and Ninja
Librarians

The library at Public School 40 had become like a second home to Caramel Parks. He loved to read as much as he loved solving mysteries. The school library had just been renovated. Two new floors and a small auditorium had been added so the school could sponsor visits by famous authors. To top that off, some rich folks from the community had donated about a zillion new books to the library's collection. That, of course, meant Caramel was happier than a ghost in a haunted mansion. More books equaled more smart snacks for his hungry brain.

Caramel sat at his favorite table in the corner of the second floor. He liked that spot because he could do his research in relative privacy. The little corner table had a computer on it, and Caramel used it to do Internet research on upcoming cases. Caramel also had a computer in his room at home, but it was good to be where the books lived.

As usual, Caramel's table was stacked sky high

1

with books. Notebooks, pens and sticky notes took over whatever remaining space that was left. He had already taken several pages of notes from the four books he had just read. All the books were about Black cowboys in the West. One focused on the famous Buffalo soldiers who helped to defend the West. Another was about the famous Black mountain men who helped to open the West for other explorers. Caramel reached for the fifth book. This one was about Black towns in the West. He turned to the table of contents.

The sound of approaching footsteps caught the attention of Caramel's world-famous hypersensitive detective's ears. He looked up just in time to see Earnie Todd, his best friend on earth, tripping over his own shoelaces. Earnie hit the floor, sending up enough dust to form the smoke signal for 'help!'

"Send me a postcard on your next trip," Caramel laughed in a whisper.

He whispered because he respected the hush rule at the library. Besides, you had to obey the rules or Mrs. Hatcher, the head librarian, would quickly descend on you.

Earnie was the definition of clumsy so Caramel let his friend help himself up off the floor. Caramel had helped Earnie up so many times in the past that he had built up strong muscles in his arms.

"Thanks for the lack of help, as usual, Kid," said Earnie, brushing the dust off his pants and shirt.

"That's what friends are for, Earn," Caramel said, pointing to his biceps. "Did you find any books on horseback riding?"

Earnie nodded his head, swinging his backpack around from off his shoulder to his chest. He reached inside the bag but found nothing but lint. Caramel sighed and simply pointed to the floor.

Earnie smiled and picked up the books. As Earnie straightened his back, with the pile of books in his arms, he crashed into Kayin McIntyre, an exchange student from Scotland and Earnie and Caramel's newest friend. The books rained down to the floor once more.

"Ha ha, sorry about that, buddy!" said Kayin as he helped scoop up the books. "I thought you heard me coming!"

Mrs. Hatcher peeked over her counter to see what the commotion was all about. To her it looked like the boys were performing a new form of aerobics—books in the hands, books in the air, books on the floor—and so on. The boys quickly quieted down, so Mrs. Hatcher returned to her work.

3

Caramel, Earnie and Kayin whispered their greetings and took seats at the cluttered table.

"I can't believe our teacher is taking us on an overnight class trip," said Earnie excitedly. "I can't wait to see a real Black cowboy town!"

"Me either, Earn," replied Caramel. "It's gonna be the world's coolest weekend camping trip."

"I didn't know there were Black cowboys," said Kayin, scratching his red shock of hair. Since coming to the United States, he had become best friends with Caramel and Earnie. Kayin had even joined them on a few cases, making their mystery-solving duo a trio.

"It's one of those things some people want to keep hidden," offered Caramel. "Kinda like how Egyptians are also Black..."

"Or how there were Blacks who fought bravely during World War II," Earnie interrupted.

"Uh, why would anyone want to hide something like that?" asked Kayin.

"Stupidity, my friend," answered Caramel. "My father says knowledge is power. If a people don't know about their great history, it will be difficult for them to have a great future. Anyway, let's get back to business."

Caramel spun the book on the Black West

upside down so Earnie and Kayin could see it clearly.

"See, there were Black towns established in Nebraska, Kansas, New Mexico and Oklahoma."

"Why did they establish Black towns?" asked a curious Kayin.

"They wanted to get away from prejudice," Caramel answered. He began reading from the book.

"In many states after the Civil War ended, Black Americans had a very difficult time realizing their efforts to become citizens. Though they were legally free, many White Americans didn't want Blacks to enjoy the rights granted to citizens. These Whites used violence and terror to keep Black Americans from voting and buying property. To escape this blatant prejudice and violence, some Black Americans began to move out West to establish their own towns."

Caramel placed a sticky note inside the book to hold the page. He closed the book.

"Wow, it was rough back then, huh?" said Kayin, obviously moved by what he had heard.

"Sure sounds like it," Caramel responded. "On this trip, we'll get to find out for sure."

"Cool," Kayin responded.

5

"We'd better get going," said Caramel.

The boys packed their belongings and walked over to the book checkout counter. Caramel handed his library card to Mrs. Hatcher. In a flash she scanned the card, and all of his books with a ninja-like flip of her wrist. She repeated her actions with Earnie and Kayin. Then the sound of kids, somewhere else in the library, who were laughing a wee bit too loud, caught Mrs. Hatcher's radar-like ears. A stern look brought silence and the librarian/ninja smiled with satisfaction. The boys quickly filled their backpacks with the books and headed for the exit.

Chapter Two: We're History

Mr. Hudson loved teaching history at PS 40. He especially loved planning class trips. There were just ten minutes until school let out for the weekend. His next history-class-come-to-life was about to begin.

Mr. Hudson walked around his classroom, collecting permission slips from his students.

"Are you guys ready to learn about the Black cowboys of the West?" Mr. Hudson asked his eager class. He received his answer in cheers and smiles.

"Great! Don't forget—I am expecting a 10 page research paper on Black cowboys from each of you a week from Monday. Emphasis on the word 'research.' You are the brightest students in the world and I want great papers about your experience—and the research to back it up."

The reminder about the paper brought two moans and two boos. Caramel knew exactly where those two moans and boos came from. He turned to look at Sharktooth Williams, PS 40's

7

resident bully, and his weird sidekick, Creepy Timmy. Sharktooth was a mountain of a boy who looked like he could wrestle a bear and win. Creepy Timmy was just the opposite—thin as a skeleton, with spiked hair and a thin green vein smack in the middle of his forehead. Creepy Timmy looked like a punk rock version of the Frankenstein Monster.

Mr. Hudson approached Sharktooth and Creepy Timmy. Nikki, the latest girl in the class to have a crush on Kid Caramel, sat behind Sharktooth, smiling at her intended beau.

"Is there a problem with the assignment, gentlemen?" Mr. Hudson asked Sharktooth and Creepy Timmy.

"Aww, I can't write a paper, Mr. Teach, cause I'm allergic to paper," said Sharktooth, making a face. He pretended to be sick just thinking about it.

"Ummm, yeah, me too, Mr. Teach, sir," echoed Creepy Timmy. "I get hives just touching the corner of a notebook." Creepy Timmy groaned like something out of a spooky movie. The remains of a blue gummy worm stuck between his teeth showed as he groaned. Chances were that the gummy worm had been a part of his malnutritious breakfast.

"Hmmm, that's too bad," said Mr. Hudson. "I guess you guys won't be having any of the homemade ice cream and chocolate chip fudge cookies they make at the ranch where we will be staying. I hear they're the best, ever."

Mr. Hudson started to walk away when both Sharktooth and Creepy Timmy took their notebooks and pens out of their backpacks. They smiled at Mr. Hudson like two perfect little angels.

"What a bunch of knuckleheads," said Caramel to Earnie and Kayin.

Sharktooth leaned forward in his chair and growled, "I heard that, Cara-bell. You guys better watch it or there's gonna be three extra tumbleweeds at that ranch this weekend."

The school bell rang and Caramel could hear the bullies laughing all the way down the hall.

Chapter Three:
On the Road Again

Saturday morning started off with the crack of thunder, which woke Caramel up with a start. He wiped the sleep from his eyes, stretched like a panther, and walked to the window.

"Aww, man, there must be some kind of law that says it has to rain on a school trip," Caramel said under his breath as he walked to the bathroom to shower.

"Son, are you ready yet?" asked Ronald Parks, Caramel's dad, a few minutes later. He was talking through the bathroom door.

"Yup, sure am, partner," answered Caramel in his best cowboy voice.

"Earnie's dad called and he said he'll be here in an hour with Earnie and Kayin," Caramel's father said.

Caramel opened the door to the bathroom and gave his father two thumbs up. "I'll be ready in a few minutes. It's time to brush the cavity monsters into oblivion!"

Mr. Parks smiled as he headed downstairs to his home law office. Although he knew his son was quite smart, he recognized the kid that was still a big part of Kid Caramel.

After eating a hearty breakfast, Earnie, Kayin and Mr. Todd, Earnie's father, picked up Caramel, and headed to school.

A large yellow bus waited in front of PS 40. As a joke, Mr. Ritter, the bus driver, tied a cowboy hat to the hood of the bus. Ms. Rose, the science teacher, joined the class as an extra chaperone. She helped collect last minute permission slips and then passed out photocopies of factsheets about cowboys. She also gave each student a map that showed blueprints of Boseville's various buildings.

Caramel, Earnie and Kayin, whom Caramel's father had nicknamed the 'Trouble Trio,' climbed aboard the already crowded bus. The big yellow monstrosity of a vehicle was nicknamed 'Ol' Yella' by the students. Well, most of the students. Sharktooth and Creepy Timmy called it 'Ol' Smella.'

All the kids brought along packed lunches for the trip to Boseville. The Trouble Trio brought their GameBro handheld video game systems and a whole bunch of books and magazines to read.

Better to have something to read rather than have to stare at Nikki's smiling face, thought Caramel.

Soon, the yellow vehicle headed toward the highway. The trip to Boseville was officially underway. Light rain that began in the morning had turned into a thunderstorm, and huge raindrops pelted the bus like pebbles. The sky was dark with clouds. What should have been a pleasant day of green grass and blue sky had turned into a moody morning. Trees cast dark shadows along the lonely highway. A howling wind added a special effect. Click. Caramel took a mental picture of the spooky storm scene. Some of the kids sang songs to the rhythm of the rain. Others slept soundly, serenaded by the rain's rhythm.

"Hey guys, this weird thunderstorm makes a great beginning to my story for the school paper," Earnie said, looking out the window. He was nowhere near as brave as Caramel or Kayin, but he had the sharp instincts of a reporter. This made Earnie great at spotting clues. Sometimes he even found them before Caramel did.

"Yeah, the storm is kind of weird," agreed Caramel. "There's fog everywhere."

Caramel opened his map. Before he could read

it, the bus hit a pothole. Contents of a can of soda, which belonged to the kid in front of him, doused the map completely.

"We have fog like this all over the Inverness area of Scotland," said Kayin. "Remember?"

"Aye," said Caramel, his voice expertly echoing Kayin's accent. The boys laughed but a burst of thunder cut them short. They all looked at each other, and then started reading the handouts on Black cowboys Ms. Rose had passed out. Mr. Hudson had planned on giving a lecture, but the rain and thunder were too much of a distraction.

"Look," said Caramel to Earnie and Kayin. "Here's a circular inviting Black Americans from the South to come out West. Someone named 'Pap' Singleton printed it."

Mr. Hudson overheard Caramel speak.

"Benjamin Singleton was a former slave," he told the boys. "He led a number of Black Americans out West where they built their own communities. That was during the 1880s. Boseville, where we're going, was founded in 1889."

Mr. Hudson put a hand on Caramel's shoulder.

"Kid, you're a detective. Maybe you can solve the case of the ghost that's supposed to be haunting the town."

13

"A ghost?" asked a startled Earnie.

"A ghost?" echoed Kayin.

Kid Caramel's brain began to percolate. He lived for mysteries. This trip was getting better and better by the minute.

Ol' Yella turned off the highway onto a bumpy dirt road. The abrupt change of terrain woke up the kids who had been sleeping.

"We're getting close to Boseville," announced Mr. Hudson.

All eyes were glued to the windows as the bus rumbled down the old road.

Caramel's eyebrows arched up when he spotted an old wooden sign posted on the side of the road. It was barely legible, but it read "Welcome to Boseville. Population 12. Plus Jake."

Chapter Four: Big Bad Barn

Mr. Ritter stopped Ol' Yella at a small booth. He rolled down the window to show the man inside the booth a piece of paper. The guard stamped the paper and returned it to Mr. Ritter. Then the guard pressed a button and an electric gate swung slowly open, allowing the bus to proceed.

Ol' Yella kicked up a wicked clod of mud and rocks as it moved up a winding path to Boseville. It was still raining. Now rocks bounced off the bottom of the bus as it lumbered along its course. Caramel imagined that the rocks were bones hitting metal.

The bus made its way to an ornate entrance sign that read "Hayes's Ranch and Rodeo." Caramel took a snapshot with his built-in Brain Camera.

"Hayes's Ranch?" asked Caramel. "I thought it was the Bose Ranch. That's strange, don't you think?"

"Aye, that is weird. I wonder if we're at the right

15

place," Kayin mused, looking at a copy of the map Ms. Rose gave them.

In response to the question that he didn't even hear Caramel ask, Mr. Hudson began explaining. "Students," he said as he stood up, "we're going to Hayes's Ranch first. That's where we'll be staying. We will visit Boseville tomorrow. There's a tour of the town already planned for us."

Caramel wasn't quite satisfied with the discrepancy in the ranch's name, but he accepted his teacher's explanation and turned to the window to take in the scenery.

As the bus headed to Hayes's Ranch, it passed a structure that looked very strange. At first glance, it looked like a barn, but it was bent way out of shape. It leaned sideways as if it was ready to tumble over. Caramel thought the building looked like something from a bad dream. The door was wide open, like a gaping mouth ready to swallow the bus whole.

Caramel squinted his eyes. "Do you guys see that? There's a man standing at the entrance. It looks like he's wearing a cowboy outfit."

Kayin stared intently at the entrance. "I don't see anything. Looks like your crazy imagination is playing tricks on you," he told Caramel.

"My imagination might be crazy, but I'm not,"

Caramel said. He switched his vision to BioScan Mode and swept the area. He saw a wooden sign near a bale of hay. It read "Horse Stables— Personnel Only." But whatever he had seen had disappeared.

Caramel turned to Kayin and Earnie.

"This is going to be a weird adventure, guys," said Caramel. "And weird is what I live for."

Finally, the bus came to a stop.

"Last stop, kids," said Mr. Ritter. "Grab your stuff and have fun! It looks like the rain stopped just in time, too."

For a brief moment, the kids on the suddenly silent vehicle snapped to attention as if they were in the military. But the silence was soon replaced by cheers, hands slapping high-fives, and the sound of dozens of feet racing to the door of the bus.

Mr. Ritter helped the students unload their luggage from the bus cargo storage. He waved good-bye and he and Ol' Yella headed for the visitor's parking lot.

All the kids looked at the building in front of them. Mr. Hudson and Ms. Rose, did too. It was Hayes's ranch.

"It's bigger than I thought," Mr. Hudson told

Ms. Rose. "And it's in better condition, too."

The students dropped their luggage and ran to peer in the windows of the ranch.

"Top bunk," Caramel called out.

"Fine with me," Earnie responded. He had no desire to sleep five feet off the ground.

Caught up in the excitement of the ranch that would be their home for the next few days, no one in the group noticed the old man who emerged suddenly from the woods.

"Hiya," he greeted in a low, raspy voice.

Caramel whipped around in one quick motion. Earnie and a few other students screamed. It wasn't every day that someone popped out of nowhere and stood instantly next to you.

The old man was dressed from head to toe in cowboy gear: chaps, spurs on his cowboy boots, and atop his head, a black Stetson hat. There was a lasso on one of his hips and a water canteen on the other. He chewed a wad of tobacco as if it were the very last piece on earth. He rolled the tobacco in his mouth, then spit tobacco juice that seemed to fly several hundred yards. The juice hit a metal garbage can. As it slid down the side of the can, Caramel imagined that the wad was melting the garbage can down into radioactive sludge.

The old cowboy looked the group up and down, and headed toward Mr. Hudson and Ms. Rose.

"You must be them folks from the city," the old cowboy said. He extended a hand to Mr. Hudson. Caramel thought his hand looked as if it had been baking in the sun for a thousand years.

"Th' name's Edwin Hayes, but my friends call me Raven Caller," the old man said. As if on cue, a real raven cawed in the distance.

Mr. Hudson smiled nervously and shook Mr. Hayes's outstretched hand. "Very nice to meet you, sir. Yes, we're the group from PS 40 in Tanwood."

"Alrighty then, folks, on behalf o' all of us here at the Hayes Ranch, welcome!" said Mr. Hayes as he stepped away from the entrance. He then yelled toward the ranch.

"Rummy!"

The door to the ranch swung open and a short, thin man appeared in the doorway. A black patch covered his left eye.

"This here's Rummy Engles, the best rodeo bull rider this side o' the sun," said Mr. Hayes. "Rummy here will help ya'll to your quarters."

Although he was thin, Rummy's hands seemed

19

as big as truck tires. He scooped up several pieces of luggage in his huge hands.

Caramel looked at Rummy standing there holding the luggage. He couldn't imagine him riding a bull during rodeos. Even a light buck and Rummy would easily go flying, Caramel thought.

Mustering a little courage, Earnie walked up to Rummy.

"Hello, Mr. Engles, my name is Earnest Todd. I'm with the PS 40 *Mirror* newspaper. Can I ask you some questions about the rodeo?"

Earnie didn't wait for an answer. He just launched into his first question.

"Did you hurt your eye while bull riding?"

Rummy just nodded and stared back at the ranch.

His interview clearly cut short, Earnie went to join the rest of the students, who were now headed to their rooms. Caramel felt a nudge as he started up the steps to the front door.

"Hey, detective-man! Aren't you going to carry a lady's bags for her?"

Caramel slapped his forehead. "No, I'm not, Nikki," he moaned. Nikki, who had the biggest crush in the universe on Caramel, rested her head on the boy detective's shoulder. Caramel quickly twisted his shoulder from under her head and walked ahead of her.

"I don't know what's gonna be worse, dealing with Nikki, or these curious characters at the ranch," moaned Caramel to himself. He looked as if he was sitting in a dentist's chair waiting for the drill.

Chapter Five:
S'mores and Spooks

Later that evening, several small campfires dotted the back yard of the ranch. Each had six to eight kids seated around it. Songs and laughter echoed in the night.

There was nothing quite like marshmallows, graham crackers, and chocolate, with wooden sticks and a campfire to cook them on.

"I've never had s'mores before," said Earnie, trying for the third time to melt the chocolate without burning his marshmallows.

"My dad and I used to make them when I was a little kid," said Caramel.

"We didn't make these either, but they sure are good," said Kayin, with half a marshmallow-covered graham cracker sticking out of his mouth.

"I'd have to say that s'mores are easily the most non-nutritious snack on earth," said Caramel, stuffing another one in his mouth.

Just then, a giant shadow loomed over Caramel, Earnie and Kayin. It was like a lunar eclipse but smelled like a moldy t-shirt, and last week's lunch.

"Well, in my book, yer all still a bunch of little twerps," said the familiar voice of Sharktooth Williams. He snickered as his partner in crime, Creepy Timmy, crawled out from his considerable shadow.

"Yeah, a bunch of wimpy twerps....hahahah, little twerrrrpsss!" echoed Creepy Timmy. He wore a t-shirt with a picture of a rat on it. The light from the campfire made the vein in his head look like a massive worm. One thing was for sure, Creepy Timmy earned his name.

"If I had known wild animals liked s'mores, I would have dropped some off at the zoo you call home," said Caramel, who wasn't scared of the school bully. Caramel and his friends started to laugh hysterically.

Sharktooth's face was less than an inch from Earnie's in the blink of an eye. He grabbed Earnie by the collar and pulled him even closer. Out of three potential punching bags, it was always Earnie who Sharktooth singled out.

"What are YOU laughin' at, you slimy twerpy ant? Sharktooth sneered, sending a drop of froth flying from his mouthful of crooked teeth. It was shark-feeding time and Earnie Steak was on the menu.

"A-ants aren't slimey, Sharktooth...they have an exo-skeleton called a carapace instead of..."

"SHUT UP, SLIME-EEEE ant!" Sharktooth bellowed, balling up his fist.

Suddenly there was an extremely loud cackle of unearthly laughter. It sounded like the Wicked Witch of the West, mixed with a sprinkle of a hyena. The laughter from another world had scared Sharktooth so badly he released his grasp on Earnie's collar and fell to his knees. Creepy Timmy jumped behind Sharktooth, using him for cover. Caramel was on his feet in a flash.

"Kid, that sounded like it came from the stables!" said Earnie as he straightened out his collar.

"Already on it, buddy!" said Caramel. He reached into his vest and pulled out his badge. He was officially on the clock.

Used to going on adventures together, the boys already had their flashlights out. They also took out their C.E.K.T.'s—short for Caramel Earnie Kayin Tracers. The C.E.K.T.'s were walkie-talkies attached to digital micro-recorders. Caramel and Earnie had invented the devices during the 'Werewolf of PS 40' case. If one of the boys got lost, the others could use the homemade gadgets to find him.

The Trouble Trio sneaked away from the group and carefully made their way through the woods.

They came to the side of the wooden barn, the same one they had seen while on the bus.

"Look, guys," said Caramel, pointing to the front of the barn. A silhouette of something with two long horns floated over the stable's double doors. Caramel and Kayin quickly turned their flashlights up toward the horned object. "It's only the skull of a steer, hung up as a decoration over the entrance," said Caramel.

"Hah!" laughed Earnie. "He says it's ONLY the skull of a steer!"

"Aren't you scared of anything, Caramel?" asked Kayin.

"Not really, as long as there's a logical reason behind it," Caramel answered. "Okay…well maybe clowns. They freak me out, but just a little bit," admitted the boy detective.

"What's the deal with clowns?" asked Earnie. He aimed his flashlight at every branch, just in case one was a tree monster in disguise.

"Clowns paint on a smile…who knows what they're really thinking," answered Caramel.

"Bro, you need mental help," said Kayin, laughing.

Kayin led the way into the barn. Three flashlight beams cut through the musty darkness of the stable. The hay on the ground felt damp, and the place smelled like wet animal fur.

They found several horses standing in individual stalls. Two of the horses chewed hay while the other one just looked at the boys as they walked around.

"I-I know something else you could be scared of," said Earnie, pointing his finger toward the center of the barn. "I-I-I think I hear something!"

"What's that noise?" asked Kayin. "It's a clanging sound."

"Sounds like spurs, the kind a cowboy wears," said Caramel.

The boys' flashlights traced the outline of a strange figure that stood at the other end of the stable. Atop the figure's seven foot tall frame sat a cowboy hat. The figure stood there for a long moment, then suddenly leaped at the three boys. Kayin and Earnie dropped their flashlights and screamed.

"What, what, what do we do, Kid?" asked a frightened Earnie.

"Just stand still," the brave detective told his friends. The figure was edging closer, but Caramel didn't want to run and lose his chance to find out what this mysterious looming figure was.

Suddenly, the entire stable lit up.

"What in tarnation is goin' on in here with all o' that hoopin' and a' hollerin'?" asked Mr. Hayes.

"We saw something," Caramel told Mr. Hayes.

"Saw what?" Mr. Hayes wanted to know.

Caramel walked to the middle of the stable. "It's a cowboy hat...but what happened to the person who was under it?"

"Oh, boy," sighed Mr. Hayes. "Looks like Mad Jake is at it again."

"Mad Jake?" asked Caramel.

"Yeah, he's the ghost that's got everybody around here scared to death. "I'll tell you about him at storytelling time."

Chapter Six:
The Legend of Mad Jake

It was eight o'clock—time to hear "The Legend of Mad Jake," as told by Mr. Hayes. The students and their chaperones were gathered in the ranch recreation room.

Caramel, Earnie and Kayin had arrived earlier than the other kids to get seats up front. They didn't want to miss a word of the Mad Jake story. Earnie, true to form, had his notebook in hand, ready to jot down juicy details. Mr. Hudson and Ms. Rose stood near the large fireplace, eager to hear what the old man had to say, too.

Mr. Hayes sat on a chair he had carved from a tree trunk. He took a deep breath, walked to the two lamps in the room and turned them off. Only the light from the fireplace kept the room from complete darkness. The old man began to speak.

"Long ago, there lived a man who had a hard life. His name was Jake Bose. His mother and father were slaves in Mississippi who were forced to work from sun up 'til sun down. After the Civil War ended in 1865, slaves were freed. But most of

28

them had no money and nowhere to go, so they became sharecroppers. Sharecroppers worked on farms. For most of 'em, the conditions weren't much better than they were during slavery. When Jake was about eighteen, he decided he was going to change his life and his family's lives too. He wasn't going to work on somebody else's farm, barely making enough to eat. He was determined to change his destiny."

Mr. Hayes leaned forward. "And that's what he did."

"Jake joined a group of other African Americans who wanted to move West. They thought the West was the best place for them to get a fresh start. There they could build their own towns and start their own businesses. Some did. There were a number of Black towns in the West, you know. But things didn't work out for the group that Jake went with. They ran out of money. They didn't have food. So Jake came up with a plan to do something about the situation. He became a bank robber."

The group cooed "ooohs" and "ahhhhs" of amazement. But Caramel wanted to hear more.

"So, Jake and his posse, the Bose Boys, began robbing banks," Mr. Hayes continued. "And they became famous, as famous as Jesse James and his gang."

29

"Did Jake make a lot of money being a train robber?" Nikki asked.

"Sure did, little lady," answered Mr. Hayes.

"What happened to Jake?" asked another student.

"The law caught up with Jake during one of the greatest shoot-outs in history!

The marshal and his deputies tracked Jake and his boys down near Moss River. That's about 100 miles from here. When the dust settled all of Jake's boys were as stiff as this here wooden chair! Ole Jake tried to swim cross that river, but he drowned."

Mr. Hayes took an abrupt and awkward bow, signaling that his story was complete. Earnie finished scribbling notes in his pad and the rest of the students applauded.

Caramel placed a stick of sugar-free banana bubblegum in his mouth and chewed it slowly. Kayin walked up to him.

"What's eatin' at you, Caramel?" asked Kayin.

"That ending just doesn't make sense," he answered as Earnie joined them.

"What connection does Mad Jake have with Boseville? Why would Mad Jake's ghost want to haunt this place?"

"Good points, Kid," added Earnie. "Maybe we'll find out more tomorrow when we visit the town."

"Maybe. But now we need to learn more about Mad Jake, to figure out what his ghost really wants," said Caramel.

"Yeah, I mean, he's haunting this place...and I'd like him to go away, or I will," said Earnie.

"Maybe if we can figure out what he's looking for, he'll stop," said Kayin.

Rummy entered the recreation room and placed a tray full of cookies on the table that sat in the center of the room. In his other hand was a pitcher of milk. He placed that on the table as well. The boys attacked the snacks like a school of piranha.

"You know what, Earn', I'm going to ask Mr. Hayes a few questions," Caramel said as he gulped down his last bite of cookie. Earnie and Kayin accepted Caramel's unspoken invitation and walked with their friend over to where Mr. Hayes was seated.

"Like my story, fellas?" Mr. Hayes asked as the boys approached him.

"Yes," answered Caramel. "But we have a few questions."

"Fire away."

"Why is Boseville named Boseville? And if Jake Bose wasn't killed in Boseville, why is his ghost here?"

"Good questions. You're a smart whipper-snapper," Mr. Hayes told Caramel. "To answer your first question, some say the town was named Boseville to show the respect the townspeople had for ole Jake. He was a hero of sorts, you know. Everybody in the West knew him. He gave money to a lot of people. He was like a Robin Hood, so to speak. Now, I don't rightly know the answer to your second question."

Kid Caramel pondered for a moment. They would need to find out more about this town, and about Mad Jake. There had to be a connection. Records? There must be records. Every town keeps records.

"Where are the town records kept?" Kid Caramel asked Mr. Hayes.

"We got a Hall o' Records somewhere in town," said Mr. Hayes. He was chewing another fresh wad of tobacco. "The only problem is, we don't know which building it's in."

"Why's that?" asked Kayin.

"Well, I bought this place three years ago. A little while after I settled in, the contents of the buildings in town started kinda randomly switching their belongings. Yup. Sometimes the stuff that's in the post office winds up in the barbershop, and vice versa. Stuff just keeps getting switched around.

"The tourists who come here probably don't believe it, but this here's a genuine ghost town! And not just 'cause they're so few of us living here either." Mr. Hayes removed his hat and used his sleeve to wipe the sweat from his forehead. "I can't keep any help. Rummy is the only one who's brave enough to stay here. He's been with me going on two years now."

"Do you know who founded Boseville?" Caramel asked Mr. Hayes.

"Some guy named Smithson. That's what I read somewhere."

"Can you take us to Boseville to do a little scouting?" Caramel asked Mr. Hayes.

"Well, I don't know. It's night and you never know when Mad Jake will show up."

"Maybe we can help you solve this Mad Jake mystery," offered Caramel. Mr. Hayes thought for a moment.

"I can drive ya'll, if it's all right with your teacher. I can show you the ole mine that spurred Boseville's growth back in the 1890s."

Excited about their new investigative opportunity, Caramel, Earnie and Kayin ran back to the recreation room where Mr. Hudson, Ms. Rose and the rest of the group were still eating.

Caramel told his teacher about Mr. Hayes's offer. At first, Mr. Hudson didn't think it was a good idea to go into Boseville at night. But Caramel persisted.

"Well, I hate to put a damper on inquisitive minds," the history teacher began. "And something tells me that if I don't allow you boys to go, you might try to sneak off, like you did earlier today," he continued accusingly.

The Trouble Trio stood waiting in silence, refusing to acknowledge their teacher's comment.

"You may go," Mr. Hudson answered finally. "But I will be accompanying you."

"I'll stay here and watch the others feed their faces," Ms. Rose told Mr. Hudson. Rummy had returned to the recreation room with a massive tray of hamburgers and hot dogs. The kids swarmed the tray like killer bees.

"Be careful," Ms. Rose warned. "This is a weird place."

Mr. Hudson smiled and nodded. "We will."

Chapter Seven: Hidden Records

The drive to Boseville didn't take long. On the way, Mr. Hayes pointed out the old abandoned mine he had told the group about. Soon, the group of adventurers, Caramel, Kayin, Earnie, Mr. Hudson, and Mr. Hayes, arrived in the center of town. Mr. Hayes turned off the car and everyone climbed out. There were no street lamps. The only light came from the partially exposed moon.

There was a chill in the night air, so Mr. Hayes gave each of the boys and Mr. Hudson cowboy hats to wear. With his badge and cowboy hat, Kid Caramel looked like a genuine western lawman. Mr. Hayes carried an old fashioned hurricane lamp and held it high over his head.

Boseville was an old western photo come to life. Old one and two story buildings, made of wood, creaked with each gust of the wind. Two long rows of buildings lined the street. The buildings had served the thriving town of settlers and workers long ago.

There was an old post office, a place to catch

the stagecoach, a small general store, and even a dress shop. In front of many of the buildings were wooden posts and railings that horsemen used to keep their mounts secure as they shopped or played cards in the old saloon.

"We can start here at the old general store," said Mr. Hayes. The green paint that decorated the building had begun peeling long ago. Like the other buildings in town, it had a wooden porch that creaked as the group walked onto it.

The inside of the general store looked like a miniature supermarket. More like a supermarket graveyard. Old cans sat on leaning shelves. Old bars of soap and sundries were scattered on several display cases. Everything in the store was coated with thin sheets of gray dust.

"We'll have to look through each and every building 'til we find what we come here for," said Mr. Hayes.

"Maybe we should split up. It would be quicker that way," Caramel suggested.

"Maybe we should NOT split up," countered Earnie.

"Aye, if Mad Jake sneaks up on us, I want to have a whole bunch of people with me to jump him," agreed Kayin. "Power in numbers."

Mr. Hudson ended the trio's discussion with an emphatic statement.

"No one is going off alone." The teacher had the final say.

Kid Caramel nodded his agreement and began scanning for clues as the entire group went from one old wooden building to the next. They searched the post office, the opera house, the saloon, the barber shop, the dress shop (the boys didn't like this one), and the stagecoach depot. But they found no records.

Suddenly, they heard a loud sound from the across the street. It sounded like something striking metal. Flashlight beams raced to the source of the sound and settled on Ezekiel's Blacksmith Shop.

"It's coming from over there," said Mr. Hayes.

The group approached the blacksmith shop. The door was already open. Kid Caramel shifted into Scan Mode, his sharp eyes surveying every detail of the large workshop. Tools of all kinds were hanging from pegs on the walls and dangling from the rafters. In the rear center of the room sat a massive furnace. In front of the furnace stood an anvil, which had a horseshoe etched on its dull metal surface.

A smudge on the anvil caught Kid Caramel's eye.

"Hmmm, this looks like some kind of charcoal substance," said Kid Caramel. He looked at the entrance, and then looked at the anvil again. He leaned over to study the angle of the smudge. By looking at it, he could tell which way the charcoal had struck the surface. He compared the angle of the smudge to where the sound came from using his patented Ultra-Sonar hearing. He tilted up his cowboy hat to see better and pointed his flashlight at the right hand corner of the workshop.

"Looks like somebody wanted us to come in here," he said.

Kid Caramel shifted his senses to Hyper Mode. The blacksmith's shop turned into a blur of details as he looked for traces of anything that didn't quite belong.

He stared at a saddle that hung on the wall. With a little help from Mr. Hudson Caramel took the saddle down and placed it on the anvil.

"There's no reason for a saddle to be in a blacksmith's shop when the saddle shop is a few doors down," Caramel thought aloud.

"Look! Where the saddle was hanging, there's a book shelf recessed into the wall!" said Earnie with amazement.

Several old ledgers sat on the makeshift shelf. Kid Caramel slid a step stool across the floor. He climbed up on it and reached up to pull one of the ledgers from the shelf. He ran a finger over the letters embossed on the cover of the ledger. His finger made a trail in the dust that covered the book.

"I think I found something interesting," said Kid Caramel."This cover says 'County Records: A-K, 1889-1925.' I think this is a list of citizens who lived in the town during that time."

The group gathered around a wooden desk to read the ledger. The desk was so old it looked like it would crumble if someone stared at it too hard. Mindful of the book's age, Caramel carefully flipped through the pages, until he reached the Bs.

Caramel mouthed the names of the people in the "B" section.

"Borley...Bormwell...Borne...Bowe. There is no Bose here. It doesn't look like Mad Jake was a citizen of Boseville. Let's keep looking. Maybe we'll find some other important documents."

The group left the blacksmith shop and continued their search, combing through every building until they reached the last one in town. Above the door's entrance hung a sign that swung

39

slowly in the wind. The first letter on the sign, a capital 'M,' was upside down, held on by a single nail. With the other letters, the upside down 'M' spelled 'Warshal's Office.'

"What in the world is a warshal?" asked Earnie.

"Earnie, the Clue Phone is ringing and it's for you," laughed Caramel. "It's the marshal's office, the law man in town."

Kid Caramel aimed his flashlight at the doorknob and reached for it. But the door slowly opened on its own. Fighting an urge to jump back a few steps, Caramel popped a piece of bubblegum into his mouth to calm himself down.

The smell of ancient paper, mold and dust made him wonder when someone had last opened this door.

The office, darker than a black hole, wasn't very large at all. "This is nothing like the police stations of today," Caramel mumbled to himself. This office couldn't hold more than thirty people standing from end to end.

Mr. Hudson's flashlight glimmered against something hanging on the wall. It was an oil lamp.

"I wonder if this lamp still works," Mr. Hudson said as he reached for the lighter he brought with him to ignite firewood. He tilted the lamp slightly to reach the wick and it caught the flame from the lighter. The room, now bathed in a warm yellow glow, revealed another lamp on the other side of the office. Mr. Hudson lit that one as well.

Caramel noticed that Mr. Hudson's shoes, which had been very shiny, were now covered in a layer of black dirt.

"Looks like your shoes are going to need some serious shoe polish, Mr. Hudson," Kid Caramel said with a smile.

Mr. Hudson looked down and noticed the soot for the first time. "A whole can of polish," he responded with a laugh. "The oil lamps must have been filled with ash and spilled onto my shoes when I tilted them," he explained.

Caramel nodded and smiled to his teacher, but raised an eyebrow to himself. There were no ashes on the floor where Mr. Hudson was standing.

Faded, tattered reward posters were tacked all over the walls. The posters offered cash rewards to anyone who could catch a wide assortment of train robbers, stagecoach robbers and bank robbers.

"There sure were a lot of thieves in the 1800s. Didn't anybody hear of a job back then?" joked Caramel as he looked for clues.

"Probably no more than there are today," Mr. Hudson explained. "The majority of people were hard working and honest. It just seems like there were a lot more robbers back then because they got a lot of attention."

"Like the news today," Earnie offered. "There's such a focus on the negative, you might think there is nothing good going on."

"Exactly," Mr. Hudson said.

One of the yellowing posters offered 5,000 dollars for the capture of the train robbers known as the Wilton Gang. Another offered a reward of 25,000 dollars for the capture of the notorious outlaw Ben Williams. Both posters, and many of the others, noted that the reward could be collected whether the criminals were brought in dead or alive.

"Now that's what I call a win-win situation," laughed Kayin, as he pointed to the phrase printed on the bottom of the poster.

"Look here!" said Mr. Hayes excitedly. "I found a wanted poster of Mad Jake underneath that table. It says 'Wanted! Dead or Alive!' And there's a $10,000 reward."

"He was mean looking," quipped Earnie.

"Sure was," seconded Kayin.

"Let's keep searching," Caramel said. "Maybe we'll find something else."

At the back of the office were two jail cells, each one just big enough to hold one person. The bars of the cells were terribly rusted and the locks were filled with grime.

A gun rack, still filled with old rifles, sat hoisted on the wall. In front of the gun rack was the marshal's desk, which was cluttered with books, paperwork, a chess set, and a worn out leather holster. To the side of the marshal's desk was the deputy's desk. That was cluttered with junk too.

Caramel and the gang crowded around to look at a photograph of two men, armed to the teeth. Sitting low on their hips were worn leather holsters that held two guns each.

"Look at this!" announced Caramel, looking at the writing below the picture. "It's the town marshal. His name was Edward Smithson. That's his deputy, a Native American man named Kohana, standing next to him."

"The marshal looks familiar," Earnie observed, carefully pulling the picture across the desk toward himself. Kayin leaned in.

"Wait a minute," Kayin said and disappeared under the nearby table. He resurfaced dusty, holding the wanted poster of Mad Jake.

"He looks like Mad Jake," Kayin announced with pride.

43

"Maybe Mad Jake is related to the man who founded Boseville," offered Mr. Hayes.

Caramel looked at the photo more closely.

"You know what, guys, Edward Smithson and Mad Jake Bose are the same person."

"You're right," Mr. Hudson said. "They sure are."

Caramel was still thinking. There was something else familiar about those two pictures.

"There's a letter sticking out from that book over there on the floor," said an excited Kayin.

Caramel picked up the book and pulled the letter from between its pages.

"Check out the photo taped to the letter. It's an older Jake Bose shaking hands with a guy named Lewis Adams. It says here that Lewis Adams helped to found one of the first Black colleges. I can't read which college, though. The print is too faded. But look, Jake is presenting him a check. And there's that name again—Edward Smithson."

Earnie took the letter from Caramel's hands. "Here, let me read it."

"I have to say that it is indeed an honor and a privilege this fine day for me to meet a person who I think will become a most influential gentleman. Mr. Lewis Adams is another Negro

44

man who will help to return our people to our former glory. Sure, it's going to be rough going. We've got a lot of dust to shake off and we're sure to endure a lot of sweat and tears. But I have to do what I can to help.

"I really don't think I can tell anyone where I got my funds. But if we're to pick ourselves up, we must have money. We've been done a mighty wrong in this country.'"

Earnie looked up from the letter.

"It ends there," he said. "Jake must not have finished writing it."

"Wow, this is pretty interesting," said Mr. Hudson.

"Jake called himself Edward Smithson. I wonder why?" wondered Kid Caramel.

Earnie started to put the letter back into the journal. As he did, an envelope fell out. Caramel opened it carefully.

"It's a deed," said Caramel. He read it.

"It's a deed to the original Boseville settlement."

"Lemme hold onto that deed, little feller," said Mr. Hayes. "I'll put it up for safe keeping." He'd been quiet until this point, but the kid detective's latest find gave him something to say.

Before Kid could hand over the deed, the lamps blew out, leaving the marshal's office in total darkness. No one could see a thing, not even a hand in front of their face.

"Kid?" Earnie called for his friend. "Kayin, Mr. Hudson....anybody?" he trembled.

A hand plopped down on the young reporter's shoulder.

"Ahhhhhhhhhhhhhhhhhh!" he screamed. "Mad Jake!"

Caramel had to suppress his laugh.

"Earn,' it's just me," Kid Caramel revealed.

"And me," added Kayin.

Earnie's sigh of relief filled the pitch black room.

"Where are Mr. Hudson and Mr. Hayes?" Earnie asked.

"Mr. Hudson," Caramel called out. There was no answer.

"Mr. Hayes?" Still no answer.

"We'd better get out of here," Kid suggested. The Trouble Trio began carefully shuffling toward the door, relying on Kid's Brain Camera to lead the way. But suddenly they stopped short.

A tall figure towered in the doorway. The entire

body of the figure was glowing! The spurs it wore clanged as the figure moved slowly on the wooden floor toward the scared adventurers. He tilted his glowing head back and let out a laugh like a madman!

"HA! HA! HA! HA! HA! HA! HA! HA! HA! HA! HA! HA!"

Caramel, Earnie and Kayin screamed at the tops of their lungs and scrambled like rats abandoning a sinking ship. But the nearly seven foot tall madman was laughing so loud he drowned out their noise.

The boys watched in terrified awe as the looming figure streaked across the room in a glow of neon green. Then, without warning, it lunged at the boys and snatched the deed right out of Kid Caramel's hands.

The boys could do nothing but scream.

Then a different kind of glow slowly began to illuminate the room. The boys turned to see their teacher standing in the corner holding a lit lamp. When they turned to point out the mysterious figure, it had disappeared.

"Mr. Hudson, where were you?" Kayin trembled.

"Looking for this," the teacher responded,

holding up the lamp as proof.

Out of nowhere, Mr. Hayes reappeared in the room. Beads of sweat dotted his forehead. He was clearly exhausted.

"The deed—it's gone," Earnie reported. "Mad Jake took it."

"That deed belongs to me," Mr. Hayes protested through long breaths. "It's a historic document. Dag nab it, that Mad Jake. I've got to find him."

"Wait, Mr. Hayes," called Mr. Hudson. "I'll look with you. You shouldn't go out there by yourself."

He relit the second lamp, and took the first one with him.

"You boys stay here," the teacher told Caramel, Earnie and Kayin as he rushed after Mr. Hayes.

Caramel looked at Earnie. Earnie looked at Kayin. Earnie had long since dropped his pen and notebook. But it didn't matter. Even with a brilliantly written article, no one would believe what had just happened.

Chapter Eight: Showdown at the Not OK Corale

"OK, guys, we have to think fast, and we're talking speeding train fast!" said Caramel. "There's an answer to this," he said as he looked around the room.

"I was studying the map of the town on the bus when that can of soda ate it. That map showed blueprints of each of these buildings. On the blueprints—what did those red lines signify?" asked Caramel, his mind working at warp speed.

"I don't think so great when I'm scared, guys," Earnie whined. "I don't remember and I think I'm gonna pass out!"

"I had a chance to read my map," said Kayin. His eyes closed tightly in thought. "Those lines were entrances to hidden passageways," he announced, careful to keep his triumphant revelation to a whisper. The boys didn't want to call any attention to themselves and risk inviting another visitor.

49

"Of course! Old buildings like this always had secret passageways!" said Caramel excitedly. "That...that...ghost or whatever it was must have gone out through one of them."

Kayin scanned the room, comparing it to what he saw on the map. "Over there, on the wall behind the deputy's desk," said Kayin, pointing to the spot. "A passageway should be right behind it!"

The boys scrambled on hands and knees toward the deputy's desk. Kayin grabbed the legs of the desk and pulled it away from the wall. Caramel pressed a small button on the bottom of his personally customized flashlight. A small screwdriver slid out of the base.

Despite their care to keep quiet, the click of the screwdriver's release caught the ears of Mad Jake on the other side of the room. He spun his head toward the sound and waited for another sound to give away the boys' location in the dark room.

Unaware that he and his friends had company, Caramel continued with his plan. He used the flat edge of the screwdriver to pull open a panel on the wall. He quietly placed the panel on the floor and motioned for Earnie and Kayin to go in ahead of him. Like an elite squad of ninja, the boys made their way into the secret passage.

Earnie, clumsy as always, tripped on the panel, stumbling into the dark passage. All three boys opened their mouths in shock as they heard the spurs of cowboy boots click toward them.

Caramel crawled into the passage as quiet as a mouse, and pulled the panel back into place.

Three beams of light illuminated the man-made tunnel. The walls were covered in charcoal dust. Hundreds of tiny green specks peppered the tunnel walls.

"Looks like the walls are coated in charcoal. I think this tunnel might have been used by mining cars," Caramel whispered.

Caramel beamed his flashlight ahead to see the tunnel's end.

"Look, there's a door," he said.

When the boys reached the end of the passageway, Kayin used his shoulder to knock the door open. A cloud of black dust billowed out of the tunnel and into the street.

When the dust cleared, the boys found themselves in the middle of town. Then the sound of laughter straight out of a nightmare filled the air. The laugh echoed into the night.

"HAHAHAHAHAHAHAHAHAHAHAHAHAHA HAHAHAHAHAHA!"

The boys stopped in their tracks—well, except for Earnie, who, still unable to control his feet, crashed into Kayin. The impact sent Kayin sprawling into Caramel, and all three boys soon found themselves in a heap on the ground. A long shadow of a tall figure wearing a cowboy hat stretched halfway across Main Street, covering the boys with its cold chill. Another laugh, this time one that could freeze steel, bellowed from the shadow's owner.

"HAHAHAHAHAHAHAHAHAHAHAHAHAHA HAHAHAHAHAHA!"

"Those secret tunnels were dug out by my own townsfolk, fellas. Don't you think I'd have other tunnels to beat you to the surface?" a voice rumbled.

"Uh-oh. Mad Jake," said Earnie. He, Caramel and Kayin scrambled to their feet. Earnie immediately spotted something that worried him even more. Caramel saw it too.

"A ghost with a gun," Caramel declared in a voice that exhibited more disappointment than fear.

The looming monstrosity's hands slowly moved down to his gun belt, ready to draw the two glowing pistols at his hips.

"We didn't come here to have a gunfight with

you, Mr. Bose," said Caramel.

Mad Jake tipped his booted toe in the dirt and dragged his foot to make a line.

"This ain't about guns, little man. Guns never make a man a man. This is about heart," said Mad Jake.

The glowing cowboy laughed into the night sky. "Step across this line to see the truth."

Kid Caramel stuck his chest out, balled his fists, and stepped forward. He took ten more steps and crossed the line.

"I already know the truth about you, Mad Jake...or should I say, Rummy."

Caramel's revelation stopped Rummy dead in his tracks. He glared at the boy detective.

"I see that your reputation as a skilled investigator is well earned, Caramel. The kids said you were good at picking up details."

"How did you know it was Rummy, Kid?" asked Earnie.

"It was just a matter of deduction, Earn."

"Easy for you to say," muttered Earnie.

Caramel began to explain.

"Thanks to my trusty Brain Camera, I noticed the strong resemblance between Rummy and the photo on the wanted poster of Mad Jake," Caramel explained.

"Sharp, extremely sharp," said Rummy, removing the glowing mask and cowboy hat. He stepped down from the stilts that made him over a foot and a half taller.

"And your last name isn't Eagles, is it?" asked Caramel. "It's Bose."

"Bose?" repeated Kayin quizzically.

"Yes, my last name is Bose. I'm one of the last surviving members of the Bose family. I came to claim my great-great-great grandfather's property. This is his town. He founded it.

"I was hoping to scare old man Hayes away. But he wouldn't leave. You see, my great-great-great grandfather founded this town to help Black people. He wanted a place where Black people could come to live without fear, and with hope. I wanted this town to reflect his legacy."

"So, Edward Smithson and Jake Bose were the same person," Caramel confirmed.

"Yes. They thought my great-great-great grandfather drowned in the river when the lawmen cornered him. But he didn't. He was a good swimmer. He survived, changed his name to Smithson, took the money he had stolen and bought this land. A lot of Black folk came here from the South. Great-great-great-granddaddy Jake helped everyone he could. He wasn't a bad person. He was a good person. You know, Boseville almost had three thousand citizens. It was a thriving center with all kinds of businesses, farms..."

"What happened to it?" Kayin interrupted.

"Back in the 1920s there was a lot of racial tension. One day, some of the White people in a neighboring town came to Boseville and set fire to it. Most of the buildings burned down except the ones that are still standing. The citizens had a difficult time rebuilding, especially once the Great Depression came in 1929. And the criminals were never punished. So, people in Boseville just started to leave."

"Why did your great-great-great-grandfather name the town Boseville? Wasn't he afraid that people would find out who he was?" Caramel asked.

"Smart," Earnie quietly complimented his detective friend.

"The townspeople did that. They wanted to show their appreciation for what he had done for them."

"But what about the glow?" asked Kayin.

"Simple," Caramel answered. "Fluorescent dust. You can get it at any costume store or magic shop."

"What's going on here?" asked Mr. Hudson, rushing up to Caramel, Earnie, Kayin and Rummy. Mr. Hayes followed behind him.

"What are you doing here, Rummy?" Mr. Hayes asked.

"I think Rummy has something to explain," Caramel told Mr. Hudson and Mr. Hayes.

"Well, I was the ghost," said Rummy, embarrassed.

"You?" a stunned Mr. Hayes asked.

"Yes, me. I'm a Bose. Boseville is rightfully mine. Great-great-great-granddaddy Jake risked his life many times to get the money to start this town and help its people."

"You mean, you're related to Jake Bose?"

"Direct descendant," Rummy replied with pride.

"Rummy, why didn't you get a lawyer to help you legally?" asked Mr. Hudson.

"I didn't have any money. This was the only way I could think of."

"My father is an attorney. Maybe he can help

you," suggested Caramel.

"Really?" asked Rummy excitedly.

"Well, I tell you, I'm a little tired of running this place," Mr. Hayes revealed. "Maybe Rummy and me could be partners."

No one was more surprised at the offer than Rummy.

"Partners!" Rummy beamed again.

"I'm getting too old for the kind work that's required to run this place," Mr. Hayes said.

"Wow....partners," Rummy considered.

"We better get back to the ranch," Mr. Hudson said. "We have a full day ahead, and these two have a lot to discuss."

Earnie smiled at Kid Caramel.

"Another case solved, huh, Kid?" he whispered to his partner.

"Yeah, Earn,'" said Caramel. "But this was a tough one."

The Trouble Trio, Mr. Hudson, Mr. Hayes and Rummy all piled into the old station wagon and headed back to the ranch.

Afterward by the Author

Hi, crew! I hope you enjoyed reading the fourth Kid Caramel mystery as much as I enjoyed writing it. My wife and I did a lot of research on cowboys, ranches, stables and more to make sure each detail was authentic.

I want to thank my friend Kenn Leroy Hill, who is a Black cowboy and Hollywood stuntman. He gave us lots of great information that I was able to use in this book. We spent the entire day with Kenn at Wild West City, which is in New Jersey. Kenn played several parts during the stunt shows. My favorite was the Marshal of the City. I liked it so much, I'm signing up to play the part of a cowboy there soon!

You'd be surprised to find out how much research has to go into a book, even mystery books. Without doing my homework on the past, I wouldn't know how to write about the 1800s, Black cowboys or train robberies. We visited several real ranches and even a ghost town so you would see what really happened a long time ago.

Keep in mind, when you do your homework and papers for school, that you'll always have a better understanding of the subject matter when you do your research. Besides, it's a ton of fun!

Well, guess what? Yup, I'm writing the next books in the Kid Caramel series, so I'll be talking to you again real soon. See ya and keep reading!

Dwayne J. Ferguson (Hunter)

Somewhere in New Jersey, 2004

Dwayne J. Ferguson is a writer and artist, creator of the Kid Caramel™ series, and illustrator of *AFRO-BETS® Coloring and Activity Book*. He loves computer games and when he's not developing characters of his own, he enjoys teaching students how to create computer graphics. Dwayne operates his own design studio and makes his home with his wife in northern New Jersey.

Don't miss other books in the Kid Caramel™ series:

Book #1 Kid Caramel: Case of the Missing Ankh

Book #2 Kid Caramel: The Werewolf of PS 40

Book #3 Kid Caramel: Mess at Loch Ness

Tell Us What You Think About **KID CARAMEL**™

Name _____

Address _____

City _____ State _____ Zip _____

Birthdate _____ Grade _____

Teacher's Name _____

School _____

Write down the title of this book. _____

_____

Who is your favorite character in this book? Do you know of anyone like Kid Caramel? Or Earnie?

_____

_____

What mysteries or cases would you like to see in future KID CARAMEL™ books?

_____

_____

How did you get your first copy of KID CARAMEL?™ Parent? Gift? Teacher? Library? Friend? Other?

_____

Are you looking forward to the next title in this series? Why, or why not? _____

_____

Any other comments? _____

_____

Send your reply to:
KID CARAMEL™ c/o Just Us Books, Inc.
356 Glenwood Avenue, East Orange, NJ 07017